ORCHARD BOOKS
338 Euston Road,
London NW1 3BH
Orchard Books Australia
Hachette Children's Books
Level 17/207 Kent Street, Sydney, NSW 2000

First published in Great Britain in 2000
This edition published in 2014

A CIP catalogue record for this book is available from the British Library.

ISBN 978 1 40832 425 7

2 4 6 8 10 9 7 5 3 1
Printed and bound by CPI Group (UK) Ltd, Croydon, CR0 4YY

Orchard Books is a division of Hachette Children's Books,
an Hachette UK company.

www.hachette.co.uk

MICHAEL LAWRENCE

ORCHARD

chapter one

before we go any further I'd better come clean about my underpants. What I mean is, no one actually died because of them – though there's no telling what would have happened if I'd had to wear them much longer.

I blame my mother. If my mum wasn't such a fanatic about the things you wear next to your skin none of this would have happened. OK, so maybe five weeks is a little long to walk around in a single pair of pants, but I always whip them off at

5

night to give them a shot of oxygen, so what's the big deal? The morning my troubles started I'd just got out of bed and was slotting my trusty old snuggies into place for the day when Mum came in.

'Jiggy McCue!' she screeched. 'The state of your underpants!'

'Have you ever heard of knocking?' I said.

'They're disgusting,' she said. 'They're filthy. They're full of holes.'

'Mother,' I said, 'they're meant to have holes. Holes are what underpants do best. Now was there anything else or did you just come in to have a go at my holey underpants?'

'I came in,' she said, 'because I'm sick of shouting myself hoarse for you to get up. But now that I've seen the condition of those articles, I see I have some shopping to do!'

6

'Oh no,' I said. 'Not new underpants. I hate new underpants. I've told you before, underpants need time to settle in, make themselves at home, breed a little friendly mould and fungus...'

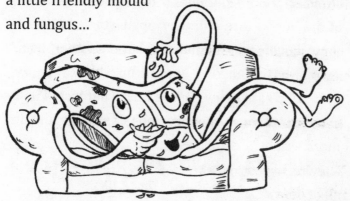

I stopped. What was the point? She was a parent. Worse than that she was a mother. Mothers don't understand these things. They also don't bother to listen half the time. 'And you're coming with me,' she said, to prove it.

'Whoa there,' I said. 'I don't do shopping, remember? Specially with my mother. It's number 47 in the Book of Rules for Good Parents I made for you and Dad last Christmas.'

BOOK OF RULES FOR GOOD PARENTS

'Put something on over those hideous things, they make me feel ill,' she said. 'We leave in ten minutes!'

'Wait!' I cried, skidding on my knees to my chest of drawers. I tore a drawer open, started chucking things over my shoulder. 'I have another pair, I know I have. Bingo!' I jumped up, shook my other cosy old pair of holey underpants in her face. 'I'll just change into these, then we don't need to go and buy more – right?'

'Yes, you will change into them,' she said. 'Then I'll at least have the comfort of knowing that if you get knocked down by a bus you'll be in clean underwear.'

I sighed. 'You miss the point,' I said. 'I mean I'll wear these *instead* of us buying new ones. I'm saving you money. Why throw the stuff away on new pants when I still have a spare pair? Do we have a deal?'

'No,' she said. 'We don't. Get changed. We're going to the market!'

And with those ten simple words my fate was sealed. The worst week of my life so far was about to begin.

chapter two

no self-respecting eleven year old boy wants to be seen shopping with his mother, right? Known fact. Why? Because when you're out shopping with the old dear you always – but *always* – bump into someone you know just as she's patting your cheek or smoothing your hair down or something. My dad doesn't go a bundle on shopping with Mum either, but at least she keeps her hands off his cheeks and hair.

'Why do I have to tag along?' Dad asked, the Saturday morning she made us both go to the market with her.

'I thought you might like a new shirt,' Mum said.

'I've already got more shirts than I can wear in one lifetime,' he said. 'I don't need any more.'

'Well, you're getting one,' she said, and plunged into the market.

It was pretty crowded. Half my class could be there. I would need to keep my wits about me so I could jump away from my mother in a split second. It was OK being seen with Dad. With Dad you don't have to be on your best behaviour, or look presentable, or do your laces up, and he doesn't make you stand still while he holds bits of material against your chest to see if they match your eyes.

11

Well there we are, Dad and me
mooching obediently after the
family tyrant, when someone
from school comes along –
not a kid, but almost as bad.

'Hello,' said Miss Weeks.
'Joseph, isn't it? Joseph
McCue?'

'No,' I said.

'It isn't?' she said, surprised because she'd obviously
gone to a lot of trouble to memorise the really
brilliant kids' names.

'No, Miss, it's Jiggy. No one calls me Joseph.'

'Why?' she said.

'Because all my life I could never keep still, ever since
I was born – and before, according to my mum. She
says I almost kicked her to a pulp before she even
saw my face.'

She smiled. 'Jiggy it is then. And is this… Mr McCue?'

Dad had stopped traipsing after Mum at the sound of Miss Weeks' voice. Miss Weeks has a nice voice, sort of soft and musical, and she has a nice smile and lots of blonde hair, and when he got an eyeful of her my dad bounced back like a turbo-driven yo-yo.

'Call me Mel,' he gushed. 'Short for Melvin, terrible name I know, but I didn't choose it, great to meet you, and you are…?'

'Dad!' I hissed.

Did I say it was OK to be seen out with my father?

But Miss Weeks wasn't fazed one bit. She smiled in that nice way she has and stuck her mitt out. 'Erica Weeks. New Deputy Head at Ranting Lane.'

My ex-father went blank. 'Deputy Head?' He looked at the hand he was suddenly holding. 'Ranting Lane?'

'Your son's school,' Miss Weeks reminded him.

'Oh. Yes. Right. Erica... Erica... Nice name.'

'Weeks,' Miss said. 'I've just moved into the area with my mother.' She glanced about. 'She was with me a minute ago. I seem to have lost her.'

'You can have mine,' I said.

'Hello,' my mother said, appearing out of thin air like an unbottled genie.

The complete stranger known as Dad threw the Deputy Hand away and stuck both of his behind his back to prove they were nothing to do with him. 'This is Emily Leeks,' he said, 'Jiggy's new Heputy Dead.'

Miss Weeks smiled at Mum but didn't stop. 'I really must dash. If I don't track down my mother she'll get herself into trouble. Bit eccentric, you know.'

Dad stood watching her go. 'Nice, isn't she?' he said.

'For a Heputy Dead,' Mum said, glaring at his profile. 'But we're in luck. I've found a stall that sells shirts, and right next to it one that sells underwear.'

I groaned.

Dad jumped guiltily into line behind her and I got behind him – but not so close people would think I knew them – and we set off once more on our quest for the underpants that were going to make me wish I'd never been born.

chapter three

The stall that was about to turn my life into a nightmare looked like something out of a fairground. It was bright red with gold stars all over it and it had a big sign on top which said *Neville's*.

It didn't take an Einstein to work out that this was the name of the owner, a dumpy little man in a red bowler hat and yellow waistcoat. He was a real grin-merchant, this Neville, but his grin was one of those insincere switch-on, switch-off types. The sort you buy in joke shops in a packet labelled 'Bad Grin'.

Mum made Dad hold a shirt against his chest from the stall next door while she ransacked the underpant section on Neville's stall. As I hung back trying to look cool, this little old biddy in a shawl hobbled by. She caught me giving her the once-over and darted towards me.

'Buy my lucky heather?' she said.

I looked down at this basket of purple stuff.

'Bring you luck,' the ancient crone said. 'Just a coin or two and good luck will follow you wherever you go.'

I chuckled, cucumber cool. 'I make my own luck.'

'That's a shame,' she said. 'Because great and terrible things are in store for you, and my heather might have protected you from the worst that is to come.'

'Great and terrible things?' I flipped my collar up to cover the hairs that had just stood to attention on the back of my neck.

'I have the Eye,' she said.

'Sorry to hear that,' I said.

'Great and terrible things,' she said again, and then once more, probably for luck: 'Great and terrible things.'

'Hey, this has been nice,' I said. 'Must do it again. Bye now.'

'Beware the very next thing you touch,' the little old woman said.

'I'll do that,' I said, and turned away laughing coolly.

'What do you think of these, Jiggy?' my mother said, thrusting something soft into my hands. 'One hundred per cent jersey-cotton. Your size.'

Suddenly I was holding a one hundred per cent jersey-cotton multicoloured horror story.

'Mum. They're horrible.'

'Well you're having them,' she said fiercely.

I looked up, all set to argue – but didn't. My mother's eyes were all red and bulgy, which they weren't usually. I glanced round for the little old gypsy lady but she'd disappeared. Maybe before she went she passed the Eye on to my mother because I turned down her lousy lucky heather.

Mum turned to Neville the Badly Grinning Stallholder.

'We'll take these,' she said.

I turned to look for Dad for moral support. He wasn't there. He must have waited till my mother was concentrating on me, then dumped the shirt and made a run for it – to a pub, knowing him.

'Mu-um,' I said in a whiny little voice.

She ignored me and handed the horrible underpants to Neville, who put them in a bag. As he gave the bag to my mother in return for her money, he turned the Bad Grin on me. I shrank back. The way he *looked* at me! Terrifying.

★★★

When we got home I was instructed to change into the new pants but take a shower first and get clean. So I went to the bathroom, locked the door, turned the shower on, and sat on the toilet reading a comic till I felt enough time had passed. Then I flicked some water at the bath towel to prove I'd used it and unfolded the new underpants.

I didn't like them any better at second glance than at first. They had this swirly-whirly pattern all over them which made your head spin. Even the label was weird. It was on the outside, on the front – and printed back-to-front.

LITTLE DEVILS

But – with a heavy sigh – I stepped into the new pants. Right foot, left foot, then the big upward haul, bend the knees for the last little lift, wriggle the hips to introduce the pantaloons to the hardware, and there they were, home.

But then something happened. Something that doesn't usually happen when you put new undies on. They shrank to fit. Gave the personal places a sort of hello hug and forgot to let go. I felt like a cling-filmed fruit bowl.

But it was at bedtime that I began to realise I had a problem. I was stripping off to jump into my PJs and catch the fast train to Dreamworld, and everything went smoothly enough till I got down to the pants.

They wouldn't budge.

They absolutely refused to drop, no matter how hard I tugged. My blinding new underpants with the dyslexic designer label clung to me like a second skin.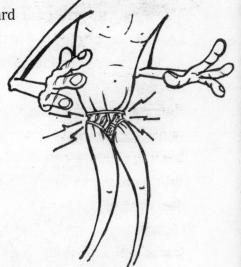

A second skin that wouldn't come off.

chapter four

When I woke up next morning I still couldn't get the new pants off, but at least they had the decency to open at the front a tad when my legs crossed, and let me drop them (but only just enough) when my eyebrows started to knit. Afterwards though, they immediately snapped back into place and nothing would shift them till my next dash to the bathroom. It was as if they had a mind of their own.

SNAP!

I decided to inform the Golden Oldies that my underpants were holding me prisoner. Dad would have been first choice to tell, but he was out playing three-a-side football with five other hooligans, which he does every Sunday morning because he's insane. That left Mum.

I'd heard her singing downstairs earlier, so the odds were she was in a better mood today. I put my dressing-gown on and went down to the kitchen. She was loading the washing machine, which is one of those things she does really well. I tell her this all the time so she won't try and get me to do it.

'Mum, you know my new pants?'

'Yes. Are they comfortable?'

'Comfortable. Well. See, there's this thing...'

'Thing?'

'Mmm. I can't seem to get them off.'

'Now don't start that again, Jiggy. I want your pants changed daily, and that's all there is to it. That is, I will do once I get you some more. Can't think why I only bought the one pair. Silly really.'

'No, you don't understand,' I said.

'Oh yes I do. Typical boy. Hate the idea of cleanliness. You wait till you start getting girlfriends.'

I gripped the edge of something and closed my eyes. Why is it that conversations with your parents always swing wildly off course a heartbeat after they've started?

'Mother. Listen. Concentrate. The new hector protectors. They're stuck to me. I mean literally. As in superglue.'

'Stuck to you? But you've hardly worn them.'

'I thought it might be something in the material, like static.'

'They should be all right,' she said. 'I know I got them from the market but they weren't particularly cheap. Perhaps they'll work loose during the day. I'm just slipping next door, Janet says she has some heathers for me.'

She opened the door and went out.

'Thanks for all the help and sympathy!' I yelled after her.

I decided to take advantage of my mother's absence and have a proper go at getting the new pants off. I draped my dressing-gown over the bread-bin and stood there in my full glory: Underpant Man! I looked around for inspiration. 'Ah-ha,' I cried, and sprang at the fish slice.

I set to work easing the cold flat end into the band of my pants. The plan was to get it right down inside, push the handle away from me, and loosen the pants just enough to slip them off.

That was the plan.

But as I tried to force the fish slice inside, the band tightened. Tightened so much I had to lift my ribcage almost to the ceiling to grab some breath. I whipped the fish slice out. The band loosened. I breathed properly again.

Then I had another idea.

I slipped a piece of string through the flap at the front of the pants and worked it up to the band on the inside. Then I looped it round and tied a good strong knot and tied the other end to the door handle. Finally I stretched out on the cold phoney quarry tiles and got set to give the door the good hard kick which would make it slam and whip my pants off.

I raised my right leg, bent my knee, took a deep breath. 'One,' I said. 'Two,' I said. 'Thr—'

I stopped at 'Thr' because my mother and Janet Overton from next door were suddenly standing in the doorway gaping at me.

I lowered my leg, slowly. 'Hi.'

Mum and Mrs O just stood there holding these plant pots and feasting their eyes. My mother's eyes were bright red and almost popping out of her head, the way they'd been at the market. Janet's were brown, and shrinking rapidly to the size of raisins because she wasn't used to coming into neighbours' houses and finding the son and heir flat out on the vinyl with his gusset tied to a door handle.

'Jiggy,' Mum said in this strangely quiet voice, 'what are you doing?'

'Testing the handle,' I replied, quick as a ferret. 'Thought someone ought to find out how strong it is. And you know what? It's terrific. I'd say we have a real winner here.'

chapter five

I know when I'm on a losing streak. It's a gift I have. I needed help. It was time to call in the Musketeers.[1] I got dressed and crossed the road. It seemed wise to do it in that order.

Pete Garrett and Angie Mint aren't related, but they live under the same roof these days because Pete's dad and Angie's mum moved in together and the kids had to go somewhere.

'I have a problem,' I said when we were sitting in a circle of three on the floor of Pete's bedroom.

'Join the club,' Pete said.

---

[1] 'One for all and all for lunch' is our motto. I don't remember which of us thought of it and I'm not sure I want to in case it was me, but whenever one of us says it, we have to stand together, us against the world. Well, that's the theory anyway.

'Why, what's your problem?'

'I haven't got one,' he said.

'But you said join the club.'

'So?'

I let it go. Sometimes talking to Pete is like talking to Stallone, our cat. No, that's not fair. Stallone would be insulted.

'So what is it?' Angie said.

'Well, it's...' I began, and stopped because a funny thing had happened.

I'd come over all bashful.

Now you have to understand that Angie and Pete and I have known one another since the year dot.

We used to hang side by side in a row from our mothers' chests while they talked about last night's telly programmes. In other words we're close. But this, well…

'No offence, Ange,' I said, 'but this is man talk.'

'It's what?' she said.

'Sorta personal. Not for the ears of mixed company.'

'Since when were we mixed company? I thought we were best buds, the Three Musketeers, one for all and all for lunch.'

'We are,' I said. 'Always have been, always will be, now will you leave the room please?'

Angie jumped up. She was really angry.

'I get the message. Last place I want to be is somewhere I'm not **wanted**.'

She stalked to the door and slammed it behind her. Then there was another slam as she went into her room along the landing. Pete and I sat in a circle of two, not looking at one another. It was a tense moment. Neither of us had ever asked Angie to leave us alone before.

But then Ange put on some music and turned the volume to full and we stopped being able to hear ourselves think, which broke the tension a little. I yelled my problem at Pete and he yelled his advice back, which was to go home and close my eyes so that when I woke up I'd realise this conversation was all a stupid dream.

There was a sudden hammering at the door, which we could just about hear over the music.

'YEAH?' Pete hollered.

The door didn't open. The hammering came again, louder.

'COME IN!' Pete shouted.

It still didn't open.

Pete got up. 'Are you DEAF?' he yelled.

He grabbed the handle. Yanked the door back. Angie stood there looking so mad I threw my arms over my face.

'IS IT MY FAULT I'M NOT A BOY?' she screamed, and stormed back to her room. Her door slammed again.

Pete closed his door, quietly. He said something.

'WHAT?' I bawled over the music.

He started to repeat it but changed his mind. Reached for a scrap of paper and a felt-tip. He wrote something and shoved it at me.

Maybe you ought to tell her,

the note said.

I took the felt-tip and wrote:

Would you tell a girl if you had a problem with your underpants?

Pete read this and took his pen back. The music stopped suddenly as he was writing.

He handed me the note.

She's not exactly a girl,

it said.

She's Ange.

I turned the paper over and wrote:

It's still embarassing.

He wrote:

Yeah well.

I wrote:

Why are we still writing when it's gone all quiet?

He wrote:

Beats me.

'Stay here,' I said, with my voice.

'Right,' he said, with his.

I left Pete and walked along the landing to Angie's
bedroom. The door was open. She was sitting
on the bed, fists
clenched, scowling
at the carpet.

'Can I come in?' I asked.

'No.'

I went in. 'Can I sit down?'

'No.'

I sat down. 'You can hit me if you like.'

'I wouldn't soil my hands,' she said.

'No, go on, hit me, you'll feel better.'

She thumped my shoulder
with a fist like a rock. My
nose hit the carpet.

'Man talk!' she snarled.

I got up, holding my
wounded shoulder. 'I
shouldn't have said that,'
I said. 'Fact is, I need your
help, Ange.'

'Well, why don't you ask **Pete**?' she said bitterly.

'I did. Shoulda known better.'

There was a shy little knock on the open door. 'All
buds again?' Pete said.

I looked at Angie. 'Buds again?'

'Only if we don't have secrets.'

'Deal.'

I held my hand out. She hesitated, but then held hers out too. 'One for all and all for lunch,' we said as we did the secret handshake. (I'd tell you about the secret handshake but then it wouldn't be secret any more, so forget it.)

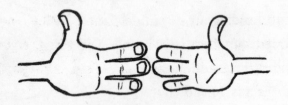

I told her about the pants that wouldn't let me take them off. I even told her about the fish slice, though I gave the string and door handle tragedy a miss. I'd just about finished and was about to ask her what she thought I ought to do, when Pete said:

'Underpants.'

'Yes, Pete,' I said, 'that is the topic of the day.'

'I was just wondering why they're called that,' he said. 'I mean why underpants?'

'Why is a house called a house?' I said. 'Why is milk called milk? Why are you called airhead?'

'No, I mean why underpants? Why not under*pant*? I mean it's only one thing, right, like a shirt? You don't say a pair of shirts, do you?'

'You might if you had two,' I said, 'and they matched.'

'You couldn't have a pair of under*pant*,' said Angie. 'Sounds stupid.'

'Yeah, but that's what I'm saying,' said Pete. 'It should be *an* underpant, like *a* shirt.'

'It's probably to do with the number of leg holes,' Angie said. 'Two leg holes equals pants. One leg hole might equal pant, but where would you put the other leg?'

'A shirt has two arm holes, though,' Pete pointed out.

'Well, that's true,' said Angie.

'Heavy stuff,' said Pete.

'Yeah,' said Ange.

'Excuse me,' I said. 'Fascinating as all this is it's not getting us much closer to solving the biggest problem of my life to date.'

'What problem's that?' said Pete.

I thumped him.

chapter six

Of course I should have known that Angie would ask to see the pants. She wouldn't be Angie if she didn't. Pete laughed cruelly, made himself at home in her rocking chair, rolled up his sleeve, and got to work on a loose scab with a fingernail.

'But I'm still wearing them,' I said to her. 'That's the prob.'

'So lose the jeans, I don't have telescopic vision.'

'X-ray,' said Pete, picking and rocking, rocking and picking.

'Oh, I don't know about that,' I said – to Angie, not Pete.

She put her hands on her hips. 'Jiggy McCue, do I have to remind you that I've seen you without your nappy?'

'Not recently you haven't,' I said.

'Yeah, well I can still picture everything if I try really hard.'

'But what if your mum comes in and I'm standing here in my underwear?'

'We tell her the truth. We say you're showing us these new pants you're so thrilled with.'

'That isn't the truth.'

'She won't know that. Strip!'

I unzipped.

'Do you want the music back on?' Pete said.

'Shut up,' I said.

My jeans hit my ankles. Pete's smirk hit his ears.

'Wow,' said Angie. 'Don't you have to have a licence for things like that?' (She meant my pants.)

She strolled round me a few times. I stared at a spot on the wall. Pete rocked and picked and smirked.

'Writing on the label's back to front,' said Angie.

'Probably made in Kong Hong,' I said.

'Show me how you can't get them off.'

'How do I do that?'

'You try to remove them, and fail.'

'What if it works this time?'

'Then you don't have a problem after all.'

I wasn't too sure about this. 'Look away just in case?' I pleaded.

'But then I'll miss it,' she said.

I shuffled round, jeans hugging my ankles, till I had my back to her. Then I tried to hook my thumbs in the band of my underpants. The band tightened, trapped my thumbs, squeezed hard. My ribcage rose.

But then the band loosened a little. I dropped my ribs, welcomed my thumbs back with open hands, and turned round.

'See?' I said to Ange.

'See what? All I saw was you sticking your thumbs in your waistband and puffing your sad little chest out. Let me have a go.'

She reached for my underpants.

'Get off!' I said.

She dropped her hands. 'You're doing it again.'

'Doing what?'

'Being sexist. I bet if it was Pete trying to pull your pants down you wouldn't object.'

'I can't believe you just said that.'

'Look, let's stop messing about,' she said. 'If they come away in my hands I'll close my eyes, I promise.'

This wasn't a decision to be made lightly, so I sighed heavily before making it. 'All right, but watch where you grip or I'm calling my solicitor.'

She walked round me a couple more times like an explorer looking for the source of the Nile. 'There's more slack at the back,' she said, and grabbed me from behind.

I squealed.

She regripped (the material this time) and tugged. No movement.

She tugged again, harder. This time the pants moved, but took me with them. She had another go. Same thing.

In the next few minutes Angie swung my pants round the room several times, with me still in them. I was getting pretty fed up of smacking the wall with my palms by the time she finally let go and said: 'Know something, Jig?'

'What?'

'You got a problem.'

It was about here that I felt a ripple. In my pants. I didn't realise it till later, but this was a sign of stuff to come, like a warning.

'Hey!' I said. 'My pants are rippling.'

And they were. The ripple started at the front, then moved round, ripple-ripple, ripple-ripple. It felt weird, but it was a definite improvement on being hugged to death.

But then, just as suddenly as it started, the ripple died – and an itch got to work. This itch was like no other in the entire history of itching, running round inside the one hundred per cent jersey-cotton like an angry rat in a cage. I went after it, scratching like I'd been to evening classes in Advanced Scratching and wanted a diploma. At first Pete and Angie didn't pay much attention, thinking it was just me living up to my name, jigging around the way I do when I get agitated, or when music starts, or when it's raining, or when I'm given homework, or – well, you name it. They got more interested when I ran at the wardrobe though, and started rubbing my underpant area up and down and side to side against the edge.

'Bears do that,' Pete said.

'Rub themselves against wardrobes?' I replied, arms in the air, hips swaying, jeans round my ankles. 'I don't think so.'

'Against trees. But I bet if you gave them a wardrobe they'd be very grateful. They could also hang their fur coats in it on hot days.'

'Pete,' I said, 'will you do me a favour?'

'Name it, Jig,' he chortled.

'Go flush your head down the toilet.'

He stopped chortling, jumped up, flicked his scab at the wall, ran out of the room.

'Was it something I said?' I quipped merrily.

Angie went to the door and leaned out. 'He went to the bathroom.'

I rubbed some more. The itching was easing off.

'He just flushed the toilet,' said Ange.

'Good news,' I said.

I continued rubbing myself against the wardrobe till I was sure my pants were an itch-free zone once more. Pete returned about then. He looked a little dazed. He also looked a little wet above the neck, and there were blue streaks on his cheeks.

'I just flushed my head down the toilet,' he said.

'Why, wasn't the basin free?' said Ange.

'Jiggy told me to. He said flush your head down the toilet and I went straight to the bathroom, got down on my knees, stuck my head in, and flushed. Couldn't help myself. There was this new Loo-Blue thing in there too.'

'I don't get it,' I said. 'It's not as if I hypnotised you or anything.'

'Maybe your itchy pants had something to do with it,' said Angie. 'You started scratching just before you told Pete to flush his head, after all.'

'Yeah, but...'

'Hey, wouldn't it be a laugh if when they get itchy and you scratch, people have to do whatever you say?'

I might have answered that, but just then I caught a glimpse of myself in the wardrobe mirror. Even with my jeans round my ankles it was an impressive sight, but there was something else. I shunted closer for a better look. In the glass, the letters on the back-to-front label weren't back-to-front.

'Holy underpants,' I said.

Angie joined me at the mirror. We stood side by side reading my label the right way round. Reversed in the mirror, the back-to-front letters made proper words. These:

chapter seven

The next day was Monday. It usually is after Sunday. Monday afternoons we have Football with Rice.

Chicken with Rice would have pleased me more, but nobody asked me when they wrote the menu. Mr Rice is our sports teacher and he wears this stupid red tracksuit all the time. Mr Rice loves football, but I don't. I could never understand what people see in it. Nor could Pete at first. We started this anti-football club when we were eight but only two people joined – us – and after a while even Pete cancelled his membership and started kicking a ball about.

The girls are lucky. They have Miss Weeks for outdoor games. This really irritates Angie. Not that she wants lessons with Mr Rice. No, it's the discrimination that gets up her nose.

'Miss,' she said one day just after Miss Weeks started, 'why do we have to do netball and rounders and stuff? Why can't we play rugby and football or even boring old cricket?'

'Because you're a girl, Angela,' Miss Weeks replied.

'Don't rub it in!' Angie snapped, and stomped off.

Another thing Angie hates is having to put on this weeny little skirt that shows her knickers. I don't blame her, so would I. Miss Weeks wears the same outfit when she takes the girls, weeny little skirt, bright green knickers. The boys find this quite interesting. I mean how often do you get a chance to see a teacher's knickers? I'll tell you. Every Monday afternoon at Ranting Lane School.

Anyway, there are the girls and Miss Weeks on that side of the field jumping in the air and showing their green knickers, and here are the boys on this side kicking stupid balls about, and suddenly old Rice-cake is bellowing at me from across the pitch.

"McCue! In goal!"

Rice always bellows. The only time his sentences don't end in exclamation marks is when he's talking to Miss Weeks. Then you can hardly hear him with an ear trumpet.

'Goal?' I yelled back. 'Me? You have to be kidding, sir!'

He charged across the pitch fingering his whistle. The man in red never goes anywhere without his whistle and is always blowing it to make you jump. As he came at me I started wishing I had a personal hero to hide behind. Mr Rice is about twice as tall as anyone else on earth, with shoulders like ox thighs and a jaw like  a set square, and when he's annoyed his forehead throbs. It was throbbing now.

'What was that?!' he barked.

'What was what?'

He stood looking down at me. 'What did you just **say**, boy?!'

I stood looking up at him. 'I said "What was what".'

'I mean *before* that!'

'Dunno, sir, can't remember.'

'I'll tell you what you said, sir! You said "You have to be kidding, sir", that's what you said, sir! Now get in goal or you'll see me after showers! Ryan, make yourself useful somewhere else! Oi, you two! Hegarty! Sprinz!'

Hegarty and Sprinz were mud-wrestling in a puddle. While Rice shot off to pull them apart, Bryan Ryan sauntered out of the goal so I could saunter in. Bry-Ry gave me this all-superior half-amused look that said, you're gonna regret taking my job McCue.

Now that I was in goal, Mr Rice planned to make the most of my terrific skill and interest. He told everyone to stand in a line facing me. The first six all had a ball at their feet. Ryan was one of them. Mr Rice blew his whistle and the first ball came towards me. I raised my arms and jumped to the far right. The ball bounced in at knee height to the far left.

'Is that the best you can do, boy?!' Rice screamed.

'Just about,' I said, wheezing a bit.

'Well try harder or you'll be over there with the girls!'

'I'll go now if you like, sir.'

The next ball came right at me. I ducked just in time.

It sank into the net behind me.

'The idea is to **stop** it, McCue, not get out of its **way**!'

'Oh, really? You should have said.'

Another ball came. This time, to show willing, I flicked a finger in its general direction as it passed.

'McCue, you are useless!'

'I'm quite good at art!' I yelled back.

'Ryan! Do your stuff!'

Ryan grinned, flexed his elbows, spun round, and trotted so far up the pitch that I began to think he was going to the pictures. But then, when he was down to a dot on the horizon, he turned round and set off at a run towards the ball. I wasn't terrifically excited about this, if you want to know the truth. In ten seconds that ball would be zooming at me with enough speed to lay out an African elephant, and there was I with no choice but to stand there with my hands on my waist waiting for it.

Ryan was fifteen metres away and closing when I felt a ripple. I looked down. My shorts, which I was wearing over my new pants, were on the move. I tried dabbing at them. The ripple moved on. I followed it. Same result.

'What the hell are you doing *now*, McCue?!' roared Mr Rice.

I might have answered, but suddenly the ripple stopped and I had more important things on my mind. It began with a little tickle somewhere too private to mention and spread through my pants like chicken pox on ice until, just as Ryan's boot connected with the ball, I fell to the ground scratching like a maniac.

'McCue, you *twit*!' I heard as the ball slammed into the back of the net – slammed so hard it bounced back and hit me between the shoulder blades. Any other time I might have been a tad upset about this, but a football in the back was nothing to the misery of the mighty Itch. I writhed in the mud, stuck my legs in the air, then my back end, then jumped up to rub myself raw against the goal post.

Mr Rice jogged up. 'What are you playing at, boy?! I know you have trouble keeping still sometimes but this is ridiculous!'

I threw myself across his enormous trainers. I wriggled between them. I got on all fours to scratch against his leg like a dog against a lamp-post. He bawled something from on high (don't ask me what, I wasn't listening). I replied with the first thing that came into my head, which I also didn't listen to. But then something weird happened. The moment I said whatever it was, my favourite sporty type spun round and sped away across the field.

After a while the itching eased off and I was able to focus on bits of the outside world. The bit that most appealed to me contained a long red streak running round the field at breakneck speed. Mr Rice. And he wasn't only running. He would run for about five metres then jump in the air, run five metres, jump in the air, run five metres, and so on. Somewhere in all this his whistle must have got stuck in his mouth and started paying rent, because every time he jumped it gave a little shriek. So what we had now was run-jump-whistle, run-jump-whistle, run-jump-whistle, all round the field. Everyone stopped what they were doing to watch, including Miss Weeks and the girls.

Pete joined me as my torment shuddered to an end.

'What's the Rice Pudding up to?'

'Must have finally boiled over,' I said, getting to my feet.

Mr Rice started to slow down. Now he was only jumping every three metres and not quite as high. Even his whistle was a whisper of its former self.

'Jig,' Pete said. 'You were itching just now, weren't you?'

'Just a bit,' I said.

'Did you say anything to Rice?'

'Might have, dunno, I was sort of distracted.'

'You can't remember what?'

'Does it matter?'

'It might. Remember telling me to flush my head down the toilet, and I had to do it, no choice?'

It came back all of a sudden, like an unwanted boomerang between the eyes. I gulped. Cleared my throat.

'What?'
said Pete.

'I told him,'
I said,
'to go take
a running jump.'

chapter eight

I'm sure Mr Rice had no idea what had made him do the running-jumping-whistling stunt round the field, but he needed someone to blame, and who better than the last person he spoke to before doing it? When he finally came to a halt he advanced on me, puffing hard, muttering my name over and over with exclamation marks. So keen was he to get his hands on me that he didn't notice Miss Weeks coming up behind him bouncing a ball, followed by her girls, who were trying very hard not to wet themselves.

'Mr Rice, that was very impressive.'

Rice froze, forehead throbbing. He heard the words before realising who said them and you could almost see him thinking **someone's pulling my stupid leg here**. But then he recognised the voice and his forehead stopped throbbing, his jaw went slack, he turned round, and became Quasimodo with neck-to-ankle blushes.

'I've never seen anyone run and jump so fast,' Miss Weeks said, bouncing her ball. 'What a marvellous example to the boys!'

Mr Rice glazed over, like my dad did when he met her at the market. It's just as well she doesn't have that effect on the boys or we'd do even less work than we do already.

'You must be very fit,' Miss W went on (again to Rice, not me).

He moved his lips around silently, reached for a football to bounce up and down in time with hers. In a dreamy sort of bark he told me and the others to go and get in the showers, and Miss Weeks told the girls to do the same, but different showers, and we all ran off, leaving the two of them alone in the middle of the field, gazing into one another's eyes, bouncing their balls in perfect rhythm.

Showers. Now tell me, why is it that boys have to shower together and girls don't? I mean Angie might feel she's being discriminated against because she has to do girlie sports and stuff, but at least the girls get separate shower cubicles. Not us. Oh no, we have to all pile in together, like it or not. Pete manages to get out of showers. He put this note together on his computer. It's got Dr Wolfe's letterhead and Dr Wolfe's forged signature and Dr Wolfe saying he must be excused because he has veronicas or something. Works a treat. Wish I'd thought of it.

I had a special reason for not wanting to shower in public that day though. So I hung back, fiddling with the muddy knot that always seems to get into my laces, till the others had stripped off and raced one another into the steam, screaming at the top of their voices. Then I kicked my boots off and started to get dressed.

And guess who trotted in.

'What's this, McCue, done already?! Impossible, lad, your hair should be wet if nothing else is!'

71

Before I could think of a decent lie, a squeaky little voice piped up from behind a locker door.

'McCue didn't go in yet, sir.'

I glared at the weed as he flashed by, shoulder blades like traffic cones, rear end like matching jamjar lids.

'Thanks, Skinner! Do the same for you sometime!'

'Get in there, lad!' Rice bellowed at me. 'And no buts!'

'No butts in showers,' I said. 'How does that work then?'

'In!'

By the time I was down to my underpants Rice was in his little office next to the changing room. I walked slowly to the showers, took a deep breath at the door, and ran in hoping the steam was dense enough to hide the multicoloured horror story glued to my beauty spots. I might have got away with it if I hadn't slipped on a bar of soap and said 'Yump!' as

I hit the tiles. As I got up, thirty eyes peered through the steam in disbelief.

'Waheeey! Looka McCue!'

'Ya godda deathwish or summing, Jig? Rice'll murder ya.'

'Rather you than me, mate. You're dead.'

I grinned all round like I knew what I was doing and stuck my head under a vacant shower while they got it out of their system. In a minute or two they'd scattered again. All except one. Eejit Atkins.

'Atkins,' I said gently, 'why are you sharing my shower?'

'Admirin' ya pants,' he said out of the side of his mouth.* 'Whereja geddum?'

I looked down, amazed. 'You like them?'

'Not 'arf. Cool.'

'If I could get 'em off,' I said, remembering to talk out of the side of my mouth, 'you could have 'em, free gift, no strings, no refunds. There's no one I'd rather give them to – 'cept maybe Ryan.' I winked at Ryan, who did not wink back. 'Or Rice,' I added, for my own pleasure.

'Or Rice what, McCue?!' boomed my hero from the doorway.

'Nice, sir,' I replied. 'I was saying how nice it is here. In these showers. At this school. With these teachers.'

---

*Atkins always talks out of the side of his mouth, unless he's talking to teachers or his mum. He thinks it's tough. Some of us talk back to him out of the side of our mouths so he won't feel stupid.

'Do my eyes deceive me?!' Rice said, hardly able to believe what they'd just picked out through the steam. 'When I say get in the showers, boy, I mean get in them naked! I do not mean get in them dressed for bed!'

I glanced down at myself and slapped my forehead. 'Silly me. Must have slipped my mind.'

I closed my eyes to listen to the water hammering on the top of my head.

'WHAT DO YOU THINK YOU'RE DOING, McCUE?!'

I peeped through my dripping lashes. Even through the steam I could see a throb starting on Rice's forehead.

'I'm taking a shower like you told me to.'

'WITHOUT THE UNDIES, BOY! WITHOUT THE UNDIES!'

'He's shy, sir,' Ryan said. 'Doesn't want us to see him without his willy warmers. Come on, McCue, get 'em off!'

There was a pause while the others considered these fine words, decided they liked the sound of them, and started repeating them.

'Get 'em off! Get 'em off! Get 'em off!'

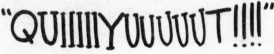

screamed Mr Rice.

The chanting stopped. The only sound was a tile falling off the wall, and the hiss of the showers as Mr Rice stepped down from the doorway. He stood at the far end, water lapping his trainers, eyes like pencil torches with my name on them.

'I don't know what your game is, McCue, but I want those things off! Now! Instantly!'

'No can do, sir,' I said. 'Sorry, but there you go.'

'WHAT?!'

'I would if I could, and that's the truth. I'd gladly stand here without my pants looking as weedy and pathetic as everyone else, but I can't. They won't let me. The pants I mean. Seems to be something in the material, and I don't mean me.'

He started towards me without the slightest concern that fierce jets of water were trained on him from both sides. Boys parted before him like the Red Sea before Moses. Next thing I know I'm being gripped by an armpit and lugged across the tiles with one shoulder on a level with the top of my head, the other trailing along behind like an unwanted relative.

Then we're out in the chilly changing room and Rice is plonking me down on a bench. He leans down and puts his nose against mine.

'You know, McCue, when I was a lad the games master would take his plimsoll to a boy for so much as walking out of step! But this is the twenty-first century and I'm obliged to be nice to you instead of giving you the thrashing you deserve! So I'm going to ask you – very nicely, very politely – to run ten complete circuits of the sports field every morning before Registration for the next fortnight!'

'Which way, sir?'

'What do you mean which way?!'

'Round the field. Or will you leave it up to me?'

'For that, lad – twenty circuits!'

'Great,' I said. 'Nice round figure. I can do ten each way.'

This must have satisfied him because he unstuck his nose from mine, jerked up to his full height, and stalked out leaving a trail of colossal footprints.

I wasn't bothered about Rice's punishment because I had no intention of doing it. No one does his punishments. They don't do them because by the next day he's always forgotten he's given them. Something to do with all the balls he's headed in his prehistoric life, that's my bet. Damaged his sporty little brain. Mr Rice has the shortest memory since…

Sorry, what was I saying?

chapter nine

It was just as well that Games was the last lesson of the afternoon, because it isn't tremendously comfortable walking round in wet pants under your trousers. Also wet patches have a way of appearing in all the wrong places, which means people call their mates and point at you. So after school I ran on home, ahead of Pete and Angie.

I went round the back as I always do, opened the gate and went up the path. There's never any problem getting in the house when the Golden Oldies are out at work, you just stick a finger in the garden gnome's bottom. My father won this gnome in a raffle. He was thrilled to bits because he never won anything before. He thought it should earn its keep, though, so he introduced the gnome's posterior to the Black & Decker, and when he finished he sat back proudly and said, 'How many burglars do you know who'd think of looking up a gnome's backside for the door key?'

First thing I did when I got in was go upstairs and kick off my damp trousers for my mum to pick up later. Then I tried a hopeful tug at the Little Devils underpants to see if the water had loosened their grip.

They shrank – dramatically.

I gasped. Stopped tugging.

They relaxed.

I plugged my mother's hair-dryer in and prayed that the pants didn't have any objection to being dry. I turned it on, aimed, held my breath. No, they didn't seem to mind.

'Hi, Jig.'

I dropped the hair-dryer. It turned itself off. Dad stood in the doorway.

'What are you doing here?' I demanded.

'I live here. I'm your father.'

'But you should be at work!'

'Afternoon off,' he said. He grinned at the hair-dryer on the floor and the underpants on me. 'I used to do that.'

I gawped. 'You had underpants that wouldn't come off too?'

'No, I just used to do that.'

Monday evenings my mother goes to her French class at the Adult Education Centre. Her French teacher is this Chinese woman called Lo-Chi or Cho-Li, I can never remember which. 'I just hope her French is better than her English,' Dad said after he met her. Mum's been going to Lo-Chi or whatever's class for about half my life and she's always saying she can't wait to try out her French in France, where they'll appreciate it. Well at last she's going to get her chance. She's arranged a romantic weekend in Paris – for one. She asked Dad to go with her, but he said she must be joking. The only foreigners my father will mix with are those who haven't beaten us at football. Mum says he might as well tear up his passport then.

Anyway, Monday evening, Mum at French class, me and Dad in the living room. I was trying to do some homework on the dining table and Dad was watching football on the telly, and the yelling was starting to get to me so much I had to ask him to control himself.

While my father shouted himself hoarse, I stared at the sheet of crosses Face-Ache Dakin, my form tutor and Maths teacher, had handed out. At the top of the page it said: *Draw quadrilaterals (four lines) round the following pairs of diagonals*. I wondered what for. Was this something you did a lot of as an adult? If not, why waste time learning how to do it at school? I mean isn't there something more useful they can teach us, like how to keep spaghetti on a fork, how to watch the stuff on TV that your parents don't want you to, how to get your underpants off?

'Dad,' I said.

He didn't answer. His eyes were pasted on the screen, where all these loons in shorts were throwing their arms round one another and kissing.

I said it again, a bit louder. He glanced at me as if I'd just strolled into church with a whoopee cushion. 'Dad, I can't remember the difference between a rhombus and a trapezium.'

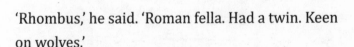

'What?' he said.

I repeated this too.

'Rhombus,' he said. 'Roman fella. Had a twin. Keen on wolves.'

'Father, this is Maths.'

'Oh, right.' His eyes darted back to the men in shorts. 'What was the other one?'

'Trapezium,' I said, without much hope.

'Roman again,' he said. 'Some sort of arena. Or maybe something to do with a circus. Trapeze, see. The word is the key. Maybe even a Roman circus. That fit?'

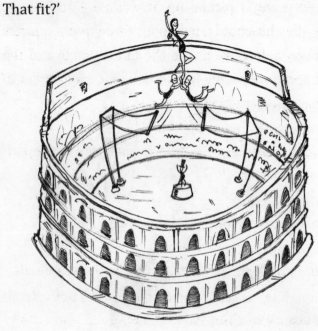

'Yeah, great, Dad. Don't know why I didn't think of it myself.'

'You only have to ask, Jig, only have to ask.'

We returned to our separate worlds for a while. But then he started shouting at the screen again and I gathered up my books and left the room.

I was halfway up the stairs when the phone on the landing rang. I picked up. It was Pete and Angie. The idle chit-chat lasted about three and a quarter seconds before we got to the Little Devils and the Itch and how people had to do what I told them to when I was scratching.

'What worries me,' I said, 'is what I do if the Itch comes on in class.'

'You try not to scratch it,' Angie said.

'Impossible. The Itch **demands** to be scratched.'

'You start scratching in class,' Pete said, 'and I ask to be excused in a hurry.'

'Correction,' said Angie. 'If Jiggy starts scratching in class, **he** asks to be excused in a hurry. Then he hares off to the Boys, bolts himself into a cubicle, and stays there till he either stops itching or gets so thin he falls in and drowns.'

'I can't go to the Boys,' I said. 'Someone might come in. Those cubicles don't have roofs, and the doors have these colossal gaps top and bottom, so if I speak the person's bound to hear me even if he can't see me.'

'So keep your trap shut.'

'Don't know if I can.'

'Yeah, you always did have a problem with that,' said Pete.

'I mean imagine,' I said. 'If I can make old Sugar Ricicles do my bidding anything can happen. I mean, like...anything.'

'Hey, that's right.' Pete again. 'You could tell him to take a stroll off a cliff. Think of it. This great red monster kicking and screaming all the way down.

We could take pictures.'

'It would be murder,' I said. 'I'd be a murderer.'

'Killer McCue,' said Pete. 'I can see the wanted posters now.'

'Wouldn't be your fault,' said Ange. 'When they haul you in front of the jury you blame your pants. They wouldn't believe you, but...'

'Yeah,' said Pete, still on his theme. 'This huge great poster nailed to trees: Wanted. Dead or alive. Killer Underpants.'

And that's how they got their name really.

chapter ten

I met Pete and Angie outside their house as usual next morning and we set off for school like on any normal day. Except it wasn't a normal day. Normal days were a thing of the past for me.

Ranting Lane is a big school, with hundreds of kids who have to change classrooms every lesson, like musical chairs without the music (and sometimes the chairs). This is so the teachers don't wear their poor old feet out coming to us. There are no lockers to stash our things in, so several times a day we have to trail round with our coats and sports gear and bags full of everything but the taps from the kitchen sink. Carrying this heavy stuff round all the time means that everyone walks with one hand trailing on the ground, even on the way to school. This is rough on kids like Eejit Atkins, who like to walk with both hands on the ground, on account of their having only just dropped down from the trees.

'Well if it ain't the Free Muskiteers.'

Atkins backed into our path from the bus shelter he'd been decorating with his spray can. We walked round him. He caught us up, fell in step, dragging a hand.

'Yoo 'ear the noos?' he said out of the side of his mouth.

'Wot noos?' I said out of the side of mine.

'We're moovin'.'

'Moovin'?' said Pete out of the side of his mouth.

'Yer. We're bein' re-'aazed.'

'Re-'aazed?' said Angie out of the side of her mouth.

'Yer. Council's givin' us a noo aarse on your estate.'

'Noo aarse?' I said.

'Wash your mouth out with soap, McCue!' bawled Mr Rice as he jogged past in his stupid red tracksuit.

Eejit loped off after some idiot buds he'd just spotted

and Angie said (out of the front of her mouth), 'What was he on about?'

'Search me,' I said. 'I don't speak Moron.'

We found out soon enough, though, because it was all round the school. You ought to know that Eejit and his older brother Jolyon and their parents lived at the end of Borderline Way, the street where Pete, Ange and I also lived till we moved to the Brook Farm Estate. Eejit's a weed, but Jolyon's a big kid, with a barbed wire tattoo where his collar should be. He used to build dustbin barriers across the road and charge kids to get in and out. Some of the parents too. No one messes with Jolyon Atkins.

Anyway, the story was this. The Council were going to pull down Borderline Way house by house, starting with the Atkins's because it's almost a ruin already thanks to the boys. That bit was OK. What wasn't OK was that they'd promised them a house on our sparkling new estate. We groaned when we heard that.

'Mr and Mrs Atkins are all right,' said Angie, searching for the bright side.

I agreed. 'Snag is,' I said, 'where they go Jolyon and Eejit go.'

'Trevor Fisher says they could move in at the weekend,' said Pete. 'He should know, his dad's on the Council.'

Angie forgot the bright side. 'The weekend? The weekend coming?'

Pete nodded.

'Well that's it then,' she said. 'By Tuesday Jolyon'll have the tiles off the roof and be flogging them at

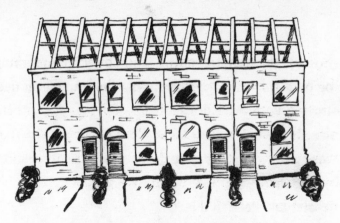

car boots. There'll be graffiti on the lamp-posts and lager cans in the bushes. Six months from now the Brook Farm Estate will be a brand new slum.'

'Still, could be worse,' I said.

'It could?'

'Sure. I mean, wherever the Council put them it can't be near us. There's a family in every house in our street.'

'Well, that's true, I s'pose...'

'Yeah,' said Pete. 'It'll be OK.'

We nodded silently together. Yep, things could be worse.

We were right.

They could.

A whoooooole lot worse.

chapter eleven

I was nervous all morning about what might happen next with the killer underpants. But the Itch didn't come, and at lunchtime I started to relax a little.

There's this place at school called the Concrete Garden where Pete and Angie and I eat our lunch most days. There are classrooms on three sides and these little concrete pigeons all over the place and a tree which isn't concrete. We have our own private bench where we swap sandwiches. Pete likes the paste ones my mother makes for me every day of my life (sardine and tomato) and I prefer his cheese and Bovrils, which he doesn't like, and sometimes we trade with Angie for her sandwich spreads because they make her throw up. That way we're all happy, even though our parents are making sandwiches for the wrong kids and don't know it.

'Geography next,' I said gloomily, feeding the lettuce from one of Pete's cheese and Bovrils to a concrete pigeon.

'Only an hour,' said Angie.

'A lot can happen in an hour. I could get the Itch and start giving orders all over the place and the school could be in smoking ruins by the end of the lesson.'

'And the downside of that is...?'

I tore my bag of crisps apart with my teeth. I was about to dip in when I noticed something that made me groan with despair.

'Oh no! She's given me spring onion now! I hate spring onion! I want salt and vinegar! I'm always telling her, don't try things out on me, I say, salt and vinegar, that's all I want, salt and vinegar, is that so hard to understand? That woman has got to go.' I offered the bag round. 'Swaps?'

They turned their backs and stuffed decent crisps into their crispholes, leaving mine to hang there watering.

Near our bench there's this little fish pond. After a hard morning at the desk it soothes the nerves to sit there watching those big gold fish weave in and out of all that weed trying to find their way home.

'I envy them,' I said.

'Envy the fish?' said Pete. 'You want gills? You want pop-eyes? You want to be painted gold and have fins and a tail?'

'They don't have underpant problems.'

'They wouldn't, they don't have anything to put in them.'

'Nice peaceful life swimming round all day, eating what they like when they want, no one bothering them.'

'No lousy lessons,' said Angie.

'No itching and scratching,' I said.

'Scratch and sniff,' said Pete.

Angie and I looked at him under our eyebrows. You

never know what's coming next with Pete.

'Your underpants,' he explained. 'They're like those scratch and sniff cards.'

'Scratch and sniff?' said Ange, pursing her lips. 'His underpants?'

'Sort of. 'Cept they're scratch and speak. He scratches, he speaks, people do what he says.'

I patted him on the head. 'Thank you, Pete. Eat my lunch like a good boy.' I worry about him sometimes.

Just then I felt something in my pants.

'Uh-oh,' I said.

'What's up?' said Ange.

'I'm rippling. Means the Itch is coming.'

'See ya!' said Pete, throwing his crisps in the air and disappearing in a puff of salt and vinegar.

Angie stayed put. She always was made of sterner stuff than him.

'Jig! Quick! To the lavs!'

'It's lunchtime!' I said. 'They'll be full of heavy smokers!'

'Well here's their big chance to give up. You order them to.'

'Here it comes!' I started to scratch. 'Oooooooooh! Agony! Murder!'

Angie put her crisps down and edged away, proving that the stuff she's made of isn't that much sterner than Pete's.

'Don't say a word!' she said.

'I'll try,' I said, scratching two-handed.

'I said not a word!'

I leapt off the bench and fell to my knees in order to rub my backside against a concrete pigeon.

'Ange,' I said.

She slammed her hands over her ears and high-tailed it. 'I can't hear you,' she said as she followed Pete out of sight. 'Can't hear you, can't hear you, can't hear you!'

I grabbed a fistful of her abandoned crisps and stuffed them in my mouth. At least one good thing had come out of this.

'Well if it ain't me old mucker McCue playing silly billies again.'

Bryan Ryan stood looking down at me from the steps of the classroom he'd been doing a detention in. There were many things I wasn't in the mood for just then and Ryan was near the top of the list.

'Take a walk, Ryan,' I said.

But then I had a thought.

A thought and a half.

'Yeah, Bry-Ry, take a walk. In the fish pond. Eat weed!'

I didn't have to say it twice. Ryan dropped his school bag and jumped into the fish pond. Splish, splash, splosh. He reached down. Goldfish swam for their lives as he grabbed their weed.

The Itch was starting to fade as Pete and Angie's heads poked round a wall to see if it was safe to return. They saw what Ryan was doing. Saw him shoving slimy fish weed past his teeth, gulping it down, shoving more in by the handful.

'Did you have anything to do with that?' Pete asked me.

I stood up, dusted myself down, shrugged modestly.

'Now that's evil,' said Angie. 'That is pure evil.'

Ryan suddenly lost interest in his latest
food fad. He looked up from the
water. His eyes were a little on the
wild side. He had all this green
stuff hanging from his mouth,
like a vegetarian vampire. He
did not look happy.

First thing I did when I got
home was strip off in my
room and go to the mirror
on the wall. The
time had come
for a heavy
talk with my
underpants, man
to gusset. OK, so I'd
had a bit of fun with old Ryan, but next time I might
not be thinking when I spoke. Next time I might do
some innocent bystander some serious damage.

'Now let's get a few things straight here, Little Devils,' I said sternly. 'You're very smart, I'll give you that. You can make people do stuff and you have a wicked sense of humour. Consider me your biggest fan. But listen, you are not a higher life-form like me. You are what the higher life-form wears round his privates to stop the world calling the cops. I say what goes, not you. I mean, yeah, you might be one hundred per cent jersey-cotton, but I'm one hundred per cent flesh, blood, bone and toenails, so no contest. Now speaking as a higher life-form to a lower one, I'm going to tell you what you have to do. You have to stop ruining my life. Got that? Do I make myself clear?'

I suppose it's too much to expect a pair of underpants to fall to your ankles and beg forgiveness, especially underpants with a mind of their own, but personally I think they overreacted a little when they shrank to about half their normal size, which made them suddenly so tight there was only one thing to do.

Stand on tiptoe and scream.

A few minutes later when they'd loosened enough for me to wipe the tears from my eyes, I noticed in the mirror that the back-to-front letters on the Little Devils label had changed. Now the label read:

'I was saying,' I said wearily, 'that you are the superior being. Number one big cheese. The underpants-that-must-be-obeyed-without-question-at-all-times. El Bosso.'

The letters changed again. This time they said:

chapter twelve

I needed a day off school. Apart from the fact that school was a dangerous place to be right now, tomorrow was Wednesday – midweek market day – and the bozo who sold the underpants to my mother might be there again. If he was there he might be able to tell me how to get the damn things off.

But you can't take time off school just because you've got better things to do. No, you have to pretend it's something else. Like illness.

'Think I'll go to bed,' I said in a faint voice halfway through tea.

'Bed?' Mum said. 'But it's egg and chips. Your favourite.'

'Feel kind of weird,' I said.

'In what way?' she demanded.

'Weak. Dizzy. Pain in my chest. Sore throat.'

'Sounds like me when my team loses,' said Dad.

'Well you go and get a good night's rest,' said Mum. To me, not Dad.

'I'll try,' I said with a small cough that said I can't promise anything, and plodded upstairs with lead in my slippers.

When I was in bed I played music very quietly till it got dark. Then I played it some more until I heard M & D coming up. I turned the music off just in time.

The door opened, ever so quietly.

'You asleep, Jiggy?'

I said nothing. Made no move.

She closed the door, ever so quietly.

I waited while they took turns in the bathroom, turned the landing light off, got into their creaky old bed. Then I waited for my mother's book to hit the floor. Her bedtime reading always falls out of her hand after ten minutes because reading in bed makes her nod off. She's been on the same book for ten months. It's a thriller.

Their lights went out. The house was dark and silent.

I waited for two more minutes before sitting up in bed. Then I let go a terrible cry of pain, thudded out of my room, along the landing, slammed the bathroom door loud enough to wake the next street but one. Then I gave this almighty roar like a werewolf ripping a sheep apart and finally raised

HOwWW

my voice in a wail of misery so tragic that the heartstrings of a charging rhino would have been plucked.

Then I flushed the toilet and waited for reactions.

There weren't any.

I opened the bathroom door.

'Mu-um?' I called feebly.

Nothing.

'Da-ad?'

Nothing.

ZZZZZZ

I dragged my poor old carcass to their door and looked in. They were asleep. Snoring.

I went back to bed.

111

★★★

To get things rolling in the morning, I didn't get up when Mum called me. Then I didn't get up when Dad called me. Then I ignored the bell. When Mum can't get an answer from me on a school day she shakes this brass handbell she keeps on a little table at the bottom of the stairs.

'Jiggy, you'll be late for school!'

'Errrrggggh,' I said.

'Are you all right?' she yelled.

'Ooooooooooh,' I replied.

She came up. I'd been rubbing my eyes to make them all swollen and my hair was all over the place and I'd wrecked the duvet and pillows. When my mother came in she found me lying with one hand trailing on the floor like a dying poet, swollen eyes trying bravely to open, lips doing their best to smile at her and croak something heroic.

'Jiggy, what is the matter?'

'Uuuuuuurrrrrrrrrrggggggh,' I said.

She felt the forehead I'd just scraped on the carpet for a minute or two.

'You're burning up,' she said.

'Waaaaa-ter,' I gasped. 'Waaaaa-ter.'

'You want some water?'

'Essss...pleeeeease.'

She went out to the landing and shouted down. 'Mel, get me a glass of water for Jiggy, he's not well!'

I heard Dad mumble something in the distance and Mum repeated the order, then came back to soothe my fevered brow and say coochie-coo things like 'There, there, it's all right, Angel, Mummy's here,' like I was suddenly half my age.

Dad hauled himself upstairs and came in with half a glass of water, and Mum asked him why only half a glass, and he said 'Tripped on the stairs, what's the matter with him?'

I groaned and Mum gripped my neck in the crook of her arm and poured water into me. I let it trickle down my chin and rolled my eyes in case she'd missed how swollen they were.

'I was so sick in the night,' I whispered huskily.

'Well why didn't you call me?' she cried, horrified to think of her little one hanging over the pan without her standing there pointlessly patting his back.

'Didn't like to…disturb you.'

She gave my shoulders a squeeze to show how touched she was. I winced bravely. And then she said the magic words.

'Well you can't go to school like this.'

'This takes me back,' Dad said.

'What does?' said Mum.

'I used to come over all peculiar when I wanted a day off school.'

Mum was disgusted. 'Mel, how could you even think that? It's quite obvious he's sickening for something.'

'Oh, he's sickening all right,' Dad said, and scooted downstairs whistling heartlessly.

My wonderful mother gazed at me with big worried eyes. 'I don't like to think of you lying here like this all day with no one to look after you. Perhaps I ought to take a day off wo—'

I jerked into a sitting position. 'NO!' I yelled.

Then I remembered I was sickening and fell back again.

'Well, if you're sure,' she said, patting her hair back into place. 'I'll bring you some breakfast on a tray.'

'I couldn't eat a thing,' I said pathetically.

'You must try, darling. You must keep your strength up.'

'No really, Mum. You go to work. I'll be all right after a day in bed, I'm sure I – cough, cough – will.'

She hesitated, but gave in. 'I'll leave the curtains closed so you can get some sleep, shall I?'

'Thanks, Mum.'

She gave me a sad sympathetic smile and went to the door, where she stood for a count of five hundred wearing a last lingering look of tragic love, and left me to it. Half an hour later she and Dad went off to work. Thirty seconds after that I was stuffing spare pillows under my duvet to make out I was fast asleep in case anyone came back and looked in on me without an appointment. Then I got dressed and went downstairs, filled my pockets with chocolate digestives, and slipped out the back way in my dad's cricket hat so no one would think I was a kid taking a break from school.

chapter thirteen

The Wednesday market wasn't as busy as
the Saturday market, but the bright red stall
with the gold stars was there again, and so was the
chubby little man called Neville, in his red bowler
and yellow waistcoat. He was still
grinning his joke-shop grin
when anyone looked his
way and still losing it the
moment they
looked away. I wasn't
sure which I preferred,
Neville grinning or
Neville not grinning.
Either way, he didn't

look like the sort you walk up to and ask for an antidote to your underpants.

'Excuse me,' I said to him. 'My mother bought some underpants from you on Saturday.'

The grin evaporated. 'You gotta complaint? Take it someplace else, I'm a busy man.'

'No,' I said, 'no complaint, it's just...well, yes, I do have a complaint actually. I can't get them off. And they make me itch.'

'Heeeeeey...' said Neville, suddenly interested. 'Are you the one that got the pants with the snappy design?'

'Yeah, that's me.'

'And they stick to you like glue?'

My pulse started to race. 'Yes! That's right! I've been wearing them for four days and nights, non-stop.'

'And they make you itch, you say?'

'Itch? I never would've believed such itches were possible.'

'And what do you do about it?' he asked.

'Do? I scratch. I have to. Like a lunatic.'

Neville tilted his bowler over his eyes and leaned closer.

'When you scratch, do you...say anything?'

I tilted my Dad's cricket hat over my eyes and also leaned closer.

'Yes! And if I tell someone to do something they have to do it!'

Neville's great unjoyous grin surfed across his chops.

'Gooood!' he said.

'What?' I said.

'They work!' he said.

'What do?' I said.

'The pants!' he said.

'You mean all that's **meant** to happen?' I said.

'You betcher!' he said.

'But it's hell!' I said.

'Fine place!' he said.

I didn't seem to be getting anywhere.

'Has anyone else bought pants like mine?' I asked him.

'No, just you. Nobody else seems to like them.'

'I don't like them,' I said. 'Trouble is I'm stuck with them. Literally.'

'Be philosophical,' he said cheerfully. 'In those pants, for the price of a small itch, you can make everyone dance to your tune.'

'I don't have a tune,' I said. 'All I want is to get them off. Come on. Please. There has to be a way.'

'Nope. Once you step into a pair of my Little Devils they're with you for life – yours or theirs, whichever lasts longest. That is, unless they come in contact with...'

He deliberately didn't finish the sentence and winked at me.

'Contact with what?' I said.

He tapped the side of his nose. 'Trade secret.'

I suddenly came over all weak.
'Why are you doing this to me?'

'Don't take it personal,'
he said. 'It could have been
anyone.'

'Anyone whose mother is
feeble-minded enough to buy
your rotten underpants, you mean.'

'So blame your old lady. Did I force her to buy them?
I think not.'

'How can you make things like this happen anyway?'
I asked.

He flipped a business
card out of his
waistcoat pocket.
Handed it to me.
I read it.

NEVILLE
THE
DEVIL
Mischief is my business

'Ever hear of a dude called Lucifer?' he said.

'Lucifer? You mean...?'

Neville nodded. 'My big brother. Started out with a bit of a complex, old Luce. The other kids called him Lucy. So he decided to stir things up a little. Did pretty well for a time. Too well. Burned himself out. Now it's my turn.'

'Your turn?'

'Yep. Neville the Devil's time has come. I'm setting up on my own.'

'With underpants?'

'I'm starting at the bottom.'

'So it's your mission in life to make mischief?' I said. 'Create havoc? For the fun of it?'

His grin reached the back of his neck. 'Couldn't have put it better myself. But a good devil has to keep his eye on the market, and seeing as no one else has your mother's fine taste in underwear from Saturday I'm switching to saucepans, frying pans, tea strainers, stuff like that. No woman can resist kitchen stuff. Soon I'll have Little Devil utensils in half the kitchens in the country. Might even start my own website.'

'What mischief can a tea strainer get up to?' I asked.

Neville the Devil's grin came a little unstuck at the edges. His eyes became shifty. 'I'll think of something.'

chapter fourteen

realising that I'd get nothing out of Neville the Devil I returned sadly to the Estate, opened my back gate, headed up the path.

And found someone in the garden, kneeling over the rockery.

Some***thing***.

'Jiggy!' the red-faced, bug-eyed monster cried when it saw me. 'But you're upstairs! In bed!'

'Um...' I said.

The monster got off its knees. I thought it was going to rush me and tear out my spleen, whatever that is, and got ready to make a run for it.

'I was so worried about you I came home from work,' the creature said. 'I went up to look in on you. You were asleep, so I thought I'd plant out the heathers Janet gave me. And all the time...'

'I just popped out for some air,' I said. 'Thought it'd make me feel better. Er, Mum,' I said, for it was she, 'what's wrong with your face?'

'My face?'

'Yes, it's sort of...horrible.'

She went into the house, still trying to make sense of me not being where she'd thought I was, and found a mirror. If this had been Hollywood instead of the Brook Farm Estate her scream would have won an Oscar.

After that, nothing could persuade my mother that I was really ill, even when I had a dizzy spell and fell face down on the couch before her bulging red eyes. She said next time she'd listen to my father, who obviously had more experience of lying and shilly-shallying than she did. She grounded me for the rest of the week (which unfortunately didn't include from school) and phoned Dad at work to tell him to come home because she thought she must have caught some fatal disease and wanted to share it with him. When Dad came in he yelped and flew back against the door. Then he bundled her into the car, wearing gloves so he wouldn't have to touch her, and drove her to the doc's by the non-scenic route.

★★★

'So what's wrong with her?' Pete asked later, as we hung around my garden. (I was allowed as far as the fence, and my friends could still come round.)

'Doctor Wolfe says she's probably allergic to heather.' I crooked an elbow in the direction of the rockery. 'Mum was planting it just before she turned into Alien 10.'

Angie wandered over to the heather. 'Doesn't look much of a threat.'

I followed her. 'It's probably not the heather. That doctor's a quack. Never gets it right with me.'

'That's because there's never anything wrong with you,' said Pete, joining us at the heather. 'Nothing a mail-order psychiatrist couldn't sort out anyway. Lucifer's little brother! Tee-hee-hee.'

I sighed. He'd been like this ever since I told him and Angie about the trip to the market.

'Errum!' I said suddenly.

Angie narrowed her eyes at me. 'Errum?'

My hips gave a jerk, all by themselves. Angie looked down. So did Pete. So did I. Something was moving in the South Pole region. My lifelong buds stepped away from me.

'Wait,' I said. 'It's different this time.'

'Tell us later,' said Pete, backing down the path.

'Over the phone.'

'It's not like the ripple I get before the Big Itch,' I said. 'It's like the pants are having a hard time of it all of a sudden. Like they're...well, not feeling so good.'

'Aw, poor things,' Pete said, keeping his distance.

'Jig,' said Angie thoughtfully. 'Remember the doc said your mum could be allergic to heather?'

'Yeah, so?'

'Well...' She nodded at the purple stuff we were standing over.

'You don't think...?' I said.

'You never know.'

I squatted beside the heather. The underpants fluttered frantically like there was a giant moth trapped inside them instead of me.

'Why didn't I think of it before?' I said.

'You didn't think of it this time,' said Ange.

'Remember the little old gypsy type at the market?' I said.

'No,' said the other two Musketeers.

'No, that's right, you weren't there. Well last Saturday, just before my mum bought the killer underpants, this gypsy woman tried to offload some lucky heather on me. Naturally I gave her the thumbs down, but then she said…what was it now…?' I rubbed my fevered temples with my fevered knuckles. Then I had it, word for word. 'She said "Great and terrible things are in store for you, and my heather might have protected you from the worst that is to come".'

'That market's obviously the place where the loons hang out,' said Pete.

'Maybe,' I said, 'but my underpants have just gone slack.'

'That must be nice.'

'You have no idea.' I stood up. 'And Neville dropped a hint that they might be beaten if they came into contact with something. He wouldn't say what, but my guess is it's heather.'

'So if you'd bought heather from the old gypsy type,' Angie said, 'you might never have had all this trouble.'

'Right,' I said. I glanced towards the house. I could hear the TV. The Golden Oldies were watching it to take their minds off Mum's face.

'Ange, look away.'

'What for?'

'Gonna take my jeans off.'

'So?'

I didn't want to go through all that again. I took my jeans off and rubbed heather between my palms and patted the material all over. Almost at once I felt something sort of like a gasp deep within my pants.

I plucked at the band. And it let me! I looked down. For the first time in four days there was a gap between the band and me. I'd never seen anything so beautiful. Angie stretched her neck to look too.

'Get outta here!' I said and let the band snap back.

'All right, I will,' she said and stalked off down the path in a huff. Slammed the gate behind her.

'She's very touchy these days,' I said to Pete.

'Women,' he said.

'Don't let her hear you say that.'

I got down on the heather, stretched out, started rolling about in it hoping the stuff would sap the strength of my pants. Pete left. I suppose it's not much fun watching someone roll around on a rockery.

In a while I stood up in the heather to see how things were going down below. The front flap was opening and closing like a vertical mouth gasping for air. I thumbed the band of the pants, tried a little downward tug. They budged.

'Yes!' I said, and tugged again.

They budged a bit more, but stuck at half mast. Still, half mast was a definite improvement on full mast and the front flap was opening and closing quite frantically now.

'Jiggy! What are you *doing*?!'

I jumped round. My mother stood in the patio doorway. I pulled my pants up, the last direction I wanted them to go. I stepped away from the heather. The band tightened round my waist. The front flap snapped shut.

'What have you done to my heathers?' Mum said.

Her eyes were almost back in her head by this time and her face was just a ripe nectarine sort of colour, but she didn't look like she planned on coming any closer just in case Dr Wolfe knew what he was talking about for a change.

'I rolled on them,' I said, and aimed a pair of irresistible cow-eyes at her. 'To teach them a lesson for what they did to my mum.'

She resisted. 'You **_rolled on my heathers_**? In your **_underpants_**?'

'I didn't want to get my jeans dirty and give you extra washing.'

She ordered me upstairs to wash the rockery off my magnificent torso and legs. I used her flannel. In spite of everything I wasn't sorry I'd taken the day off. For one thing I hadn't had the Big Itch all day. For another I'd learned that the killer underpants could be defeated – by heather. Even by the ordinary non-gypsy non-lucky variety.

I went to my room lighter of heart than I'd been all week. But I'd hardly got through the door when I felt a tug at my gusset. Then it was pulling me across the room towards the mirror. I stood watching the letters on the back-to-front label regroup. The words they became brought me crashing back to earth with an incredibly dull thud.

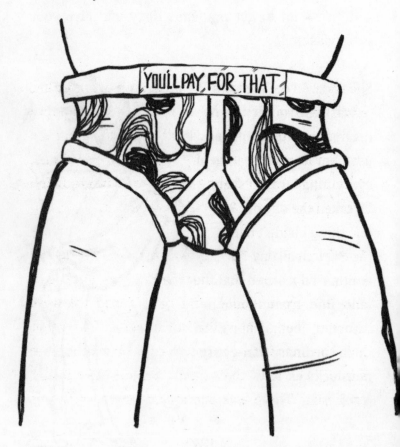

chapter fifteen

but I was in a good mood again next morning. I knew what I had to do to defeat the killer underpants. After school I was going to spend the entire hour and a half before my parents came home rolling in Mum's heather. All right, so I'd be grounded for the rest of my life, but it'd be worth it.

The first lesson of the day was Art and Design, and I don't mind that. Mr Lubelski takes us for A & D and he's from Poland, and nice. Today we were drawing feet. That is, half of us were. The other half, the ones with a bare foot each on chairs, were sitting back with their hands behind their heads, criticising. There was one major drawback to this lesson. Mr Lubelski had provided the chairs to put the feet on but he hadn't thought of providing pegs for our noses. I was drawing one of Pete's feet and I almost passed out just looking at it. The nails were rimmed with black, jagged as a rusty chain saw, and you could have hit the dirt between his toes with an arrow from the far end of the sports field. As for the smell, think cheese factory, double it, multiply it by four hundred, then ram your nose into a block of ice to stop it self-destructing.

'Jiggy,' Mr Lubelski said in his nice accent, 'do you really need to stuff tissues up your nostrils?'

'Only way to survive, sir.'

He wandered over half smiling, but when he got close I saw him go all pale and grip an easel. 'I see what you mean,' he said, and tottered to the window for a rasher of air.

Pete scowled. 'Get a move on. I don't want to sit here all day having my foot pulled to pieces.'

It was when Mr Lubelski was called away on school business that the day went all wrong. I was sitting there quietly drawing Pete's foot and Pete was sitting there quietly moaning while all hell broke loose around us.

'Sit still,' I said. 'I'm just getting the hang of that toenail.'

'Which one?'

'The black and green one with the walrus moustache. Hup!'

'What do you mean, hup?' he said.

The tissues dropped out of my nose. My underpants were rippling. Rippling like never before. Rippling so hard my trousers might have been full of bubbles. People started to notice.

'Is it what I think it is?' Pete said.

'Dunno,' I said. 'This is new.'

'Itching yet?'

'No, not...uh. Oooh! Yes, I...Oh, my...'

I hit the ground scratching. Pete's chair did a double somersault as he jumped to his foot. The class cheered. They thought we were fooling around. Copycat chair somersaults followed. Desks flew. From the floor where I was writhing I saw Pete dodging falling furniture, knocking over art materials, plunging through bundles of kids as he made for the door.

And a terrible idea came to me. An idea so disgusting and cruel that if I hadn't been rolling round the floor scratching like there was no tomorrow I would have been sitting in a strait-jacket hugging myself with glee.

To put my brilliant idea into action I needed a victim. I wasn't fussy, anyone would do. I grabbed the nearest ankle. Tugged at it. The owner of the ankle came tumbling down on top of me. I pushed him off.

It was Ryan.

Bry-Ry had been keeping his distance since the fish weed incident. Like Mr Rice after his running-jumping-whistling stunt, I don't think he understood what had happened, but he kept giving me these wild looks, half fearful, half vengeful. And now we were lying nose to nose on the floor of the art room.

No, I thought, I can't do it to him again – can I? And then I thought: yeah, course I can! I grabbed his ear.

'Wipe every trace of dirt off Garrett's foot, Ryan,' I whispered into it. 'With your tongue!'

Oh boy, was this going to be good!

'You're out of your tiny mind,' Ryan said.

I stared at him through a haze of frantic scratching. Why hadn't he jumped up and gone after Pete? Always worked before, and this time I really wanted it to work. I mean, like, *really* wanted it to work.

Ryan got up and gave me an affectionate kick in the ribs that I hardly noticed. I glanced around. Pete had stopped near the door, pretty certain now he wasn't near me that it would be someone else who got dumped on. Little did he know it, but he wasn't off the hook yet. Someone had his beady eye on him. Someone who had to wipe that foul foot clean with his tongue if it was the last thing he did.

Me. Jiggy McCue.

The killer underpants had said they'd make me pay, and they'd meant it. I was going to have to carry out my own orders!

Pete must have realised something was wrong when I started slithering across the floor towards him, because he spun round and lurched at the door. He didn't make it. I grabbed him by the heel. By the bare, nauseatingly unclean heel.

And licked it.

'Huh?' Pete said over his shoulder.

Maybe because he was so shocked, maybe because I had his foot in my mitt, he tottered and went crashing over.

His foot was even more hideous up close. Smeared with all kinds of filth, dotted with grit, fluff, slimy stuff, and – I swear on my cat's life – a squashed spider. And I had no choice but to wipe it all off. With my tongue. I got to work.

'HUH?!'

This was the rest of the class. They'd stopped trying to wreck the room. They stared in horror as...

I won't describe it if you don't mind.

My stomach heaves just at the thought of it. I was still itching like crazy, but my need to lick the dirt off Pete's revolting foot beat even my need to scratch myself senseless. It was my most miserable experience ever and I couldn't stop. Pete yelled and squealed, twisted and tugged, but I had him in a foot-lock. Nothing he did could free his foot from my grasp or keep it from my dirt-hungry tongue. I had superhuman strength. I was a kid possessed. By killer underpants.

But then, suddenly, I stopped itching, and at that same moment the need to poison myself with Pete's foot left me. I jumped up, rushed to the big white sink in the corner, and spat and spat and spat. Then I drank a jar of dirty paint water and spat and spat and spat some more.

I might have gone on doing this for some time if Pete hadn't lugged me away by the neck and shoved his licked foot in the sink and attacked it with the big wire scrubbing brush, going 'Eerk, eerk, eerk,' and shuddering so hard it's a wonder his shoulders didn't fall off. He didn't mind his feet being absolutely utterly out-of-this-world repulsive, but he got plain ill at the thought of it being wet-cleaned by human tongue.

I understand this.

chapter sixteen

pete wasn't all that keen on sitting next to me for the rest of the day. He gave the impression that even sitting in the same galaxy was a bit of a problem. He wasn't very happy about walking home with me after school either come to that, and kept ten paces behind all the way. Once again Angie showed that she was made of sterner stuff. She just walked five paces behind.

'You can't blame me, Pete,' I said, strolling backwards. 'You think I wanted to lick your lousy foot? You think it's my wish to die horribly from foot pox?'

'Did I hear a little voice?' Pete said, scanning the sky. 'The voice of someone I never want to see or speak to again?'

'Yep,' said Ange, from five paces in front of him.

I protested. 'It's the Little Devils! They said they'd pay me back for heathering them, and they did. They turned everything around, made me do what I told Ryan to do!'

'Did the same little voice of someone who no longer exists as far as I'm concerned just say that it told Ryan to lick my foot?' Pete said to the sky.

'Yep,' said Ange.

'And does this person who is now absolutely extinct seriously expect me to *forgive* him for that?' Pete said.

'Seems to,' said Ange.

I could see Pete's point. He'd been breeding a whole new strain of bacteria on that foot and I'd ruined everything. Worse still, he now had feet that didn't match. It could take years for the clean one to catch up.

'Wait,' I said.

I stopped walking backwards. Angie stopped too, five paces behind. And Pete, five paces behind her. I whipped out a pen and scrap of paper. These are the words I wrote:

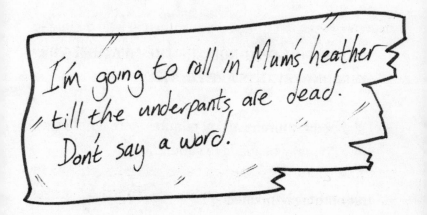

I'm going to roll in Mum's heather till the underpants are dead. Don't say a word.

I carried the note to Angie. Her lip trembled but she stood her ground and took it from me. 'Give it to Pete,' I said, and went back to my place.

Angie took the note to Pete, then returned to her place five paces in front of him. Pete read the note. Then he looked up, and said, with a snarl so loud that every pair of underpants this side of the moon could hear:

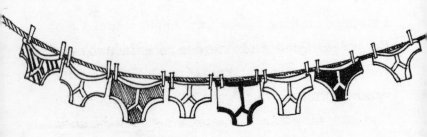

'YOU'RE GOING TO ROLL IN THE HEATHER TILL YOUR UNDERPANTS ARE *DEAD*?'

I slapped my forehead. My minutes were numbered. Now I'd really be made to suffer.

But nothing happened.

Not a thing, apart from a little flutter round my groin.

'They're probably suffering from a hangover after making you pig out on Pete's filthy foot,' said Ange.

'You reckon?' I said hopefully.

'Either that,' my ex-friend Pete said, 'or they've got something even worse in store for you and are saving their strength.'

I kicked up my heels and headed for home at speed.

Reaching the back gate, I ran up the path, slipped the key out of the gnome's bottom, flung open the door, threw my school bag on the floor, kicked my shoes off, and removed my trousers.

I was ready.

As I strolled out to the patio in my underpants I thought of the stab of pleasure I'd got when I had the idea of ordering Ryan to mop up Pete's foot. All right, it hadn't worked, my pants had turned on me, but I'd got the same bang out of telling him to do it as when I told him to eat weed. Angie had said that was pure evil. She was right. Neville the Devil was making me wicked through my underpants. I was becoming Jiggy McHyde. Also, if the Little Devils felt like a spot of extra entertainment they could make *me* do any of the stuff I ordered *others* to do.

The killer underpants had to be thwarted – right away!

Grinning mercilessly, I approached the heather patch in the rockery. The grin still hung there for a while after I noticed something I'd missed when I ran up the path to the back door.

The heather was gone!

Janet Overton next door must have heard my groan because her head suddenly appeared on top of the fence.

'Hi, Jig. Tell your mum I removed the heather like she asked in her note. Give her my sympathy. I once had an allergy to butter beans.'

I stood staring at the bare patch of earth that was no longer chock-a-block with the stuff that was going to solve everything.

'Butter beans?' I mumbled.

'They brought me out in hives,' Mrs O said. 'You like those pants, don't you?'

chapter seventeen

next morning, I'd made it halfway to the front gate when Mum called me back for my second farewell hug of the day.

'See you Monday,' she said, clasping me to her.

'Mum,' I said, 'we've done this, go inside, you're embarrassing me.'

She'd been all fond and huggy since dawn because by the time I came home from school she'd be in Paris doing the Can-Can alone. After work yesterday she'd spent a couple of hours with her Chinese French teacher getting a final French boost, and she was pretty full of herself because Lo-Chi or Cho-Li had told her that she was her best student. Dad wasn't too thrilled about the Paris weekend. He kept warning Mum against going, and when she finally lost it with him he shrugged and said, 'On your own head be it, oi revoyer and bon appeteet, and don't say I didn't warn you.'

★★★

English was the first lesson of the day. The class crashed into the English room, bags hit the ceiling, chairs and desks were scraped mercilessly to announce our arrival, a couple of fights broke out, and Mrs Gamble stood there smiling sweetly, arms folded, till we simmered down and I stuck my hand up.

'Miss, would you punish me for something I didn't do?'

'No, Jiggy, of course not.'

'Good, because I didn't do my homework.'

This always gets a laugh, from Mrs Gamble too, because she likes me and I'm pretty cool at English. But I couldn't relax, even here. The Big Itch could come any time and something I said could send someone on the rampage – maybe even me.

I stayed nervous all morning and all through lunch on my own, abandoned by two lily-livered Musketeers and forced to eat sardine and tomato sandwiches and ostrich flavour crisps.

I went on being nervous all through History. Still no Itch, but I felt sure the Little Devils were saving themselves for something.

By the time we got to Maths – last lesson of the week, yippee – I was hardly daring to hope, hardly breathing. My eye was on the clock. Tick-tick-tick. Tock-tock-tock. I'd almost made it to home time. Could my luck really hold for ten more minutes till the bell went? The little hand flicked to the next minute.

And it started.

The ripple in the dungeon under the stairs.

The warning of Things to Come.

Now nine minutes is only nine minutes to most people, but Face-Ache Dakin likes to squeeze every last second out of his precious hours with us, so he didn't give a cheerful devil-may-care grin when my right arm shot out of its socket and I started yelling that I had to go to the toilet without delay. He also didn't appreciate it when Pete clapped his hands over his ears and disappeared under his desk. When I jumped up, leapt at the door, flung it back and fled, I heard Face-Ache screaming at me to come back at once. I couldn't do

that, of course, and I didn't have time to explain, but he wouldn't have believed me anyway.

Once out in the corridor I decided to give the bogatorium a miss and hoof it home. Dakin was already going to kill me for leaving his class without permission, so there was nothing to lose.

'Where do you think you're going, McCue?!'

Mr Rice stood just outside the main office, where he'd probably been running through his athletic poses for Miss Weeks. I didn't answer. Didn't dare. Dark forces were tickling my tonsils, trying to make me say the first thing that came into my head so someone could be made to suffer.

As I hurtled out of the school gates scratching myself stupid, I tugged out a roll of masking tape I'd been carrying round all day for emergencies. I tore a strip off, slapped it over my mouth, headed down the street.

'McCue! Get back here this minute!'

I glanced back. Rice was coming after me. The poor fool didn't know what he was risking. His legs were three times longer than mine and in two minutes he'd be tearing the tape off my mouth, and when my mouth started flapping...

I approached the shopping centre all set to break the land-speed-scratching record. I ran across the square, heading for home, where I would lock myself out of harm's way and throw away the key until my pants rotted. I was almost through the square when I noticed a sign over a shop with a big front window.

A shop that sold heathers! A flower shop! The antidote was at hand!

I veered towards the shop.

'McCue! Stop right there or you – are – in – TROUBLE!'

Mr Rice was coming up fast behind me so I flung back the flower shop door and ran in, scratching insanely. There was a little woman inside, arranging flowers. I didn't dare take the tape off in case the killer underpants made me say something everyone would regret. I tried asking for heather by telepathic communication and grunts. Unfortunately the little woman hadn't done an evening course in telepathy and grunting, and instead of giving me a bunch of heather she shrieked, threw herself back against the wall, and knocked over two flower displays which toppled sideways, one one way, the other the other. Then each of them hit another, which hit another, and suddenly displays were tumbling all round the shop like falling dominoes. The terrified owner fled into a little office at the back and shoved a bolt across the door. Nothing for it then. I had to help myself. I looked round, scratching frantically. Heather... heather... where? There wasn't any. Not the tiniest bit.

And then I realised.

Heather must be the name of the woman who owned the shop!

Suddenly the world crashed. I turned. The big glass window had been struck by a tumbling display case. It was imploding in a krillion pieces. And the door beside it was opening. Mr Rice was coming in, forehead throbbing. He was reaching for me with his two enormous paws. And as he reached the itching started to run out of steam. Ten seconds and I'd be back to normal, and in BIIIIIIG trouble.

THROB!

Unless…

I barely noticed the pain as I ripped the masking tape off my mouth.

'Pay for all the damage and forget you saw me today!' I screamed at Mr Rice.

His great hams dropped to his sides. Then one of them unzipped the little money pouch he wore round his waist and took out a credit card. I looked him in the eye. It looked away. I looked him in the other eye. It also looked away. I'd told him to forget he'd seen me today, and he couldn't see me! I stepped past him. He was knocking on the office door, eager to hand his credit card to Heather, the owner.

I went home, pleased that the killer underpants hadn't turned the tables on me again. If they'd made me do what I told Rice to – pay for the broken glass and all – I'd still be handing over my pocket money at eighty.

chapter eighteen

Saturday again. Saturday morning. I phoned Pete and Angie and talked them into coming to the market with me for moral support. I needed to have another go at persuading Neville the Devil to free me from the curse of the underpants before I started World War Three.

It was still quite early by the time we got to the market, so it wasn't exactly milling with people. I led the way to the red stall with gold stars. Instead of clothing it had kitcheny stuff today, like Neville said it would, and every saucepan, tin opener, knife, fork and spoon had the Little Devils logo (the right way round).

'Hey,' Neville said, laying the Bad Grin on me. 'The ungrateful kid with the lucky underpants.'

'Excuse me?' I said. 'Lucky? Have you any idea what these things have put me through this week?'

'Sure. I know a lotta stuff. Devils do.' He leaned towards me, very close. 'This is only the beginning, kid. A month from now you could be famous. Locked up with the key thrown away, but famous. Think of it.'

My future life flashed past my eyes. I wasn't going to enjoy it. Angie stepped forward. 'Listen,' she said with a growl that I'd have to clone for my own use at the earliest opportunity, 'my friend's underpants are making his life a misery—'

'And mine,' said Pete, standing firmly behind her.

'—and whatever it is you put in them has got to be removed before something goes seriously wrong – right? Now are you going to do it or are we going to have to take this further?'

Neville heard her out. Then he gave her the Grin. 'Further?' he said. 'Like where exactly?'

'Where?' said Angie.

'Where you gonna take it? Whatcha gonna do about it?'

Angie groped for an answer, but none came. I took charge again.

'Look...sir...all I want is to get my underpants off. You needn't worry, I won't tell a soul about them. You can sell as many pairs as you like. You can kit out the entire civilised world with them, just set me free, release me, that's all I ask.'

'How selfish can you get?' Pete said from the back.

'I'm desperate,' I snapped. 'What do you say?' I said to Neville.

'I say learn to live with them,' said he. 'I say go out into the world and make mischief and bring a little joy to the jolly black heart of Neville the Devil.'

Angie jumped in again. 'Neville the Devil! Lucifer's kid brother! What do you take us for? You're a phoney. Just another market trader selling gimmicky tat, and I'm warning you...'

Her voice trailed off. It trailed off because Neville had removed his hat and we were staring at the two little warty stumps on the head underneath.

Little warty stumps that began to grow before our eyes.

That developed points.

That became horns.

Pete and Angie and I took turns to look at one another. When we'd seen enough, we nodded, spun around, and ran like stink.

They got further than I did because they didn't crash into a little old lady with a basket on her arm. I gripped the old dame's scrawny elbows to stop her tumbling into the crowd and being trampled to skin and bone. She smiled gummily up at me.

'Lucky heather?' she croaked, shoving her basket in my face.

I sniffed the purple stuff suddenly decorating my nostrils. 'Huh?'

'Hey, you! Old lady! Geddaway from here, I told you last week!'

Neville sounded upset. I glanced back just in time to see him plonk his hat on the two small puffs of smoke that hovered where his horns had been. Then I saw why he was miffed. His shiny saucepans and strainers and tin openers and knives and forks and spoons had gone dull. All of them. Some were actually turning black. The prongs on the forks were starting to wither and curl up.

'Must be the heather,' muttered Ange, who'd come back when she caught me missing.

'Yeah...' I said, feasting my eyes.

And the lucky gypsy heather wasn't only getting to the stuff on the stall either. I felt a definite sag in the cargo hold. I gave a little wriggle and rearranged the personal equipment.

Pete had also returned by this time, and the three of us stood gawping at the stall, which didn't seem anything like as red as it had been – more a pinky grey, with the gold stars turning to tarnished brass. Even Neville's clothes weren't as bright as they had been, and the man himself had gone quite pale. He was still telling the gypsy woman to get lost, but in a much smaller, weaker, almost pleading voice.

'Dracula,' said Pete.

'Eh?' I said.

'What happens when the ancient professor type holds a crucifix in front of Drac's eyes?'

'He goes a bit off-colour,' Angie said.

'He goes a *lot* off-colour,' said Pete.

'He's not too fond of garlic either,' I reminded them.

'Nor am I,' said Ange, 'but I don't curl up and die.'

'I'm talking heather here,' Pete said impatiently. 'Like heather and Neville the Devil? With me so far?'

'Heeeey,' I said.

'Exactly,' said Pete.

I spun on the old gypsy lady. 'How much for the lot?'

'Make me an offer I can't refuse,' she replied, suddenly a smart-aleck Mafia person in a shawl.

I went through my pockets and held my palm out to show her my personal fortune before tax.

'I can refuse that,' she said, and spat on my shoes.

'Angie,' I said, 'Pete. Give me your money! All of it!'

'Get outta here,' said Pete.

'This is an emergency,' I said.

'Your emergency, not mine.'

I snatched his chest, did a Rice on him, forehead to forehead, nose to nose, tried to make the veins stand out in my neck.

'Gimme your spondulicks or next time I get the Itch I send out a hit squad, and that's a promise.'

He smirked but turned his pockets out. While he was doing this I asked the little old gypsy how the Eye was. She said it was fine, thanks for asking. I showed her our combined wealth.

'Help yourselves,' she said, snatching the cash.

I grabbed a sprig of heather and shoved it inside the band of the underpants (which were loose, loose, loose).

Then the three of us each took two big handfuls of heather from the basket and advanced on the stall holding it before us like purple torches.

The closer we got, the more the kitcheny stuff withered and twisted and darkened. And as for Neville...

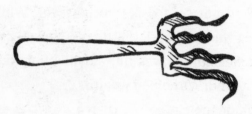

Neville the Devil started to shrivel before our eyes, hat, waistcoat and all. 'You can't do this to me,' he wailed as he shrank.

We leaned over the stall, waving heather triumphantly. He glared up at us, but he was no longer big enough to be scary. First he became a very small Neville, then a tiny Neville, then an itsy-witsy Neville. His foot slipped on something, and he went shooting into a drain, cute little hands clutching wildly. He got a grip on the grill, and hung from it.

'I'm sorry,' Angie said, 'but you have to go,' and dropped some heather on his hands.

This must have caused Neville's grip to weaken, for

when he next spoke his voice faded away to nothing.
'I'll be

baaaaaaaaaaaaaaaaaack...'

A few people had
gathered round. We'd
been blocking the view,
so they hadn't seen
Neville shrink to
Barbie's Ken size and
go down the drain.
They could see the stuff
on the stall though. The
withered, twisted, superdull
kitcheny stuff. And was it their
imagination? Hadn't this sad grey
sagging stall been bright red when they last looked?
And those grubby little blobs all over it, hadn't they
been...gold stars?

'Oh there you are, Mother!' a familiar voice said
nearby. 'I've been looking for you everywhere. Is
this disappearing act going to be a regular Saturday

market thing? And where's that heather you keep buying from the flower shop? Don't tell me you've sold it all again.'

Ducking down in the crowd, the three of us watched Miss Erica Weeks, Deputy Head of Ranting Lane School, chat to her mother, the little old woman who bought heather from the flower shop when it came in on Saturdays and sold it on to prats like me for all the money their friends had in the world.

chapter nineteen

rushing home from the market with heather still stuffed down my pants for luck, I went straight upstairs, slammed my bedroom door, put a chair against it, and breathed deeply. I lowered the killer underpants. They dropped easy as pie. Slithered all the way to the carpet without a murmur of complaint, or even a parting squeeze. A lump rose in my throat. I'd begun to wonder if I'd ever see underpants round my ankles again. I was so happy I stepped out of them and did a jig of joy around the room, whirling them round my head, singing at the top of my voice. This might have gone on for some time if I hadn't noticed the window cleaner grinning like teeth had just been invented. He raised both thumbs at me (bad move on a ladder) and lost his footing. Must have banged his chin on twelve or thirteen rungs before he hit my mother's poor old rockery.

Mum came back early from Paris. A day and a half early actually, as Dad and I were scoffing fish and chips with our fingers, feet on the coffee table, horror film on the TV. Suddenly she's standing in the doorway watching this crazed werewolf tear this innocent hitch-hiker apart.

'Mum! What are you doing here?'

In one swift movement Dad shoved the last of his chips down his neck, folded the paper over his fish bones, stopped the film, removed his feet from the table, and stood up to accept the Perfect Husband of the Year Award to a round of silent applause. Then he asked Mum why she wasn't in Paris. She didn't exactly answer, just said she was never going there again, which made Dad go all smug, though he tried not to show it.

'Rude were they, the French?' he said knowingly.

'They made fun of the way I talk.'

He put an arm round her so he could wipe his greasy fingers on her shoulder. 'So what do they know?'

Mum shrugged him off. 'They know how **French** should sound.'

'Well so do you. Should do, you've been learning it since Queen Victoria slid off the throne.'

'Yes!' she screeched, running to the door. **'With a Chinese accent!'**

I was leaving the bathroom next morning when my mother shot out of my room with the ex-killer underpants on the end of my ruler.

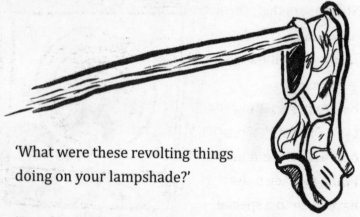

'What were these revolting things doing on your lampshade?'

'Revolting?' I said. 'I thought you liked them.'

I didn't dare tell her that her eyes were suddenly as red as sun-dried tomatoes and her face twice its normal size. I'd have to wait till she was staring in horror at the bathroom mirror to smuggle out all the lucky heather I'd stuffed under my bed last night.

Mum wouldn't allow any other dirty clothes in the washing machine with the underpants, but that suited me fine. Gave me the opportunity to sit in front of it shouting 'Take that! And that! And that!' every time they thudded over in the foam. Most fun I'd had all week. Pete and Angie spoiled things by coming over before the washing cycle finished. When I opened the front door I thought they must have been to a special Sunday clinic to give blood, because there wasn't any in their faces.

'Have you seen?' Angie said.

'Seen what?' I said.

They stood back to give me a clear view of the street. A battered old van stood on the pavement outside the house next door.

'So you don't know who's moving in?' said Ange.

'No one can move in,' I said. 'People already live there.'

'They turned out to be squatters,' said Pete. 'They were evicted overnight. You have new neighbours, Jig.'

Men were unloading things and carrying them in. One of the men was Mr Atkins. The other was his tattooed son Jolyon.

★★★

I was up in my room that same afternoon doing some homework I'd managed to hide from myself all week when some sixth or seventh sense made me go to the window. Coming across the back fence that separates us from our new neighbours was a long pole with a butcher's hook on the end. The hook was heading for the line of clothes Mum had spent the day washing instead of talking Chinese French in Paris. Reaching the line the hook found the item it wanted, tugged a couple of times, and carried my sparkling clean Little

Devils back across the fence.

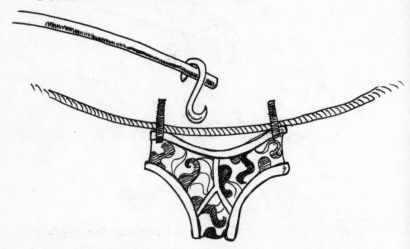

I was puzzled. What sane person would want to steal the things? But then I remembered Eejit Atkins and last Monday's showers after football when he said he thought my pants were cool and I said he could have them if I ever got them off. Well, a promise is a promise. Besides, my mother had worn out her best scrubbing brush on them before turning them over to the washing machine to be pummelled to death. Nothing could survive treatment like that. The worst damage Eejit Atkins could do with them was blind everyone when he took off his trousers in the changing rooms. "Bye-bye, killer underpants!" I chortled merrily, and returned to my homework.

chapter twenty

You won't be surprised to hear that my mother refused to believe I wasn't behind the Little Devils' disappearance. But I could live with that. I could live with anything now. I was smiling again. I was even smiling as I left the house for school on Monday morning. Pete and Angie greeted me just like the old days. Pete put his arm round my neck and squeezed. 'Hope you appreciate how I stood by you,' he said.

'One for all and all for lunch,' said Ange, and we did the secret handshake I'm not going to tell you about, and headed schoolward with a jolly air and a spring in our step. Everything was back to normal. Almost.

'Oi, 'ang abaat!'

Eejit Atkins ran out of his new house and loped across the road. Traffic swerved.

'Great innit?' he said out of the side of his mouth. 'We're neighbours agin. We kin go to school t'gevver ev'ry day!'

'Yeah that's really great, Eejit,' I said out of the side of my mouth.

'Dream come true,' said Pete out of the side of his mouth.

'Happiest day of my life,' said Angie out of the side of her mouth.

'Ere,' Atkins said as we left the estate. 'I could be the uvver Muskiteer, couldn't I?'

'Wot uvver Muskiteer?' I asked.

'That Dartanyanyan geezer. The one wot bought it at the end.'

'Pick those feet up, you lot!' cried the hearty voice of something in red as it jogged past.

'This I do not believe,' said Pete.

Nor did I. Nor did Angie. Mr Rice was not alone. There was another tracksuited type with him. He'd found a jogging partner. A Deputy Head jogging partner.

'Ooh!' said Eejit Atkins.

'You never said a truer word, Atkins,' said Pete.

But Eejit hadn't oohed because of Rice and his fellow jogger. No, it was something else. He gave a little wiggle as he walked. Then a bigger wiggle. Then his hips went all peculiar and he fell to the ground, rolled off the curb kicking the air and squealing out of the side of his mouth.

And he was scratching. Like a maniac.

'Pete,' I said. 'Ange. That's not what I used to do, is it?'

'Yeah,' said Pete.

'Exactly what you used to do,' said Ange.

'You know what this means, don't you?' I said. 'It means the killer underpants aren't dead. It means all they needed was a rest from heathering and washday. It means we'd better ruuuuuuun!!!'

Six Musketeer feet hit the pavement.

'Oi, you free!' Eejit Atkins shouted from the gutter.

We covered our ears, stared straight ahead like runaway horses with nails in their tails. Mr Rice and Miss Weeks gaped as we galloped past. So did everyone else. They'd never seen kids in such a hurry to get to school.

Certainly not this kid.

THE END